YUVAL ZOMMER

THE BIG STICKER BOOK OF THE BLUE

Thames & Hudson

This book belongs to:

....

Illustrated by
YUVAL ZOMMER

First published in the United States of America in 2018
by Thames & Hudson Inc., 500 Fifth Avenue, New York,
New York 10110

Reprinted 2019

www.thamesandhudsonusa.com

ISBN 978-0-500-65180-3

Printed and bound in China by
Everbest Printing Co. Ltd

Hello!

I am your guide, Sardine Sid.
Follow me to the deepest depths
of the big BLUE sea.

You will need: a pencil, some coloring
pens, and an imagination as big as a WHALE.

You can also get creative with the fishy
stickers at the back of this book.

Let's go!

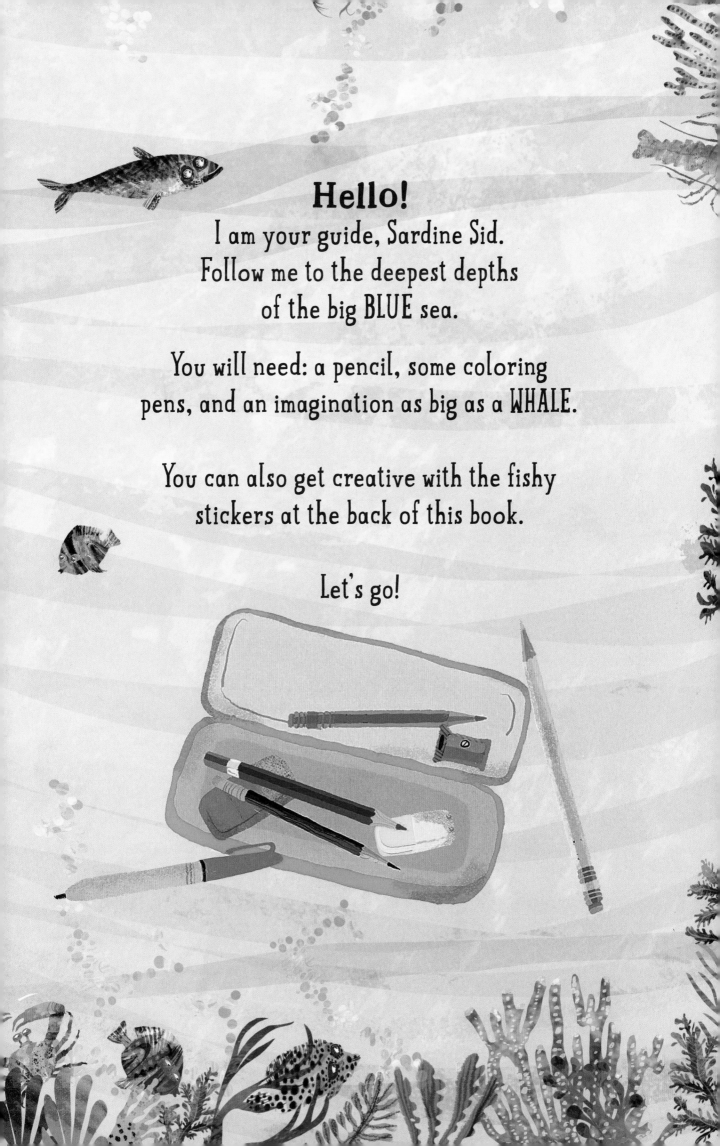

Stick flying fish in the air
and help them escape their
predators in the sea. Make sure
they don't get eaten by gulls!

Sharks have two rows of teeth
so they can eat their prey quickly.
Draw lots of razor-sharp teeth
in the sharks' mouths.

Baby sharks lose a set of teeth
inside their mother's tummy
before they are even born.

Sharks don't eat people on purpose but they have been known to mistake them for seals and big fish.

Crabs can only run sideways because their knees bend out to the sides, instead of front to back. Trace the tracks in the sand to find out which crab walked to which friend.

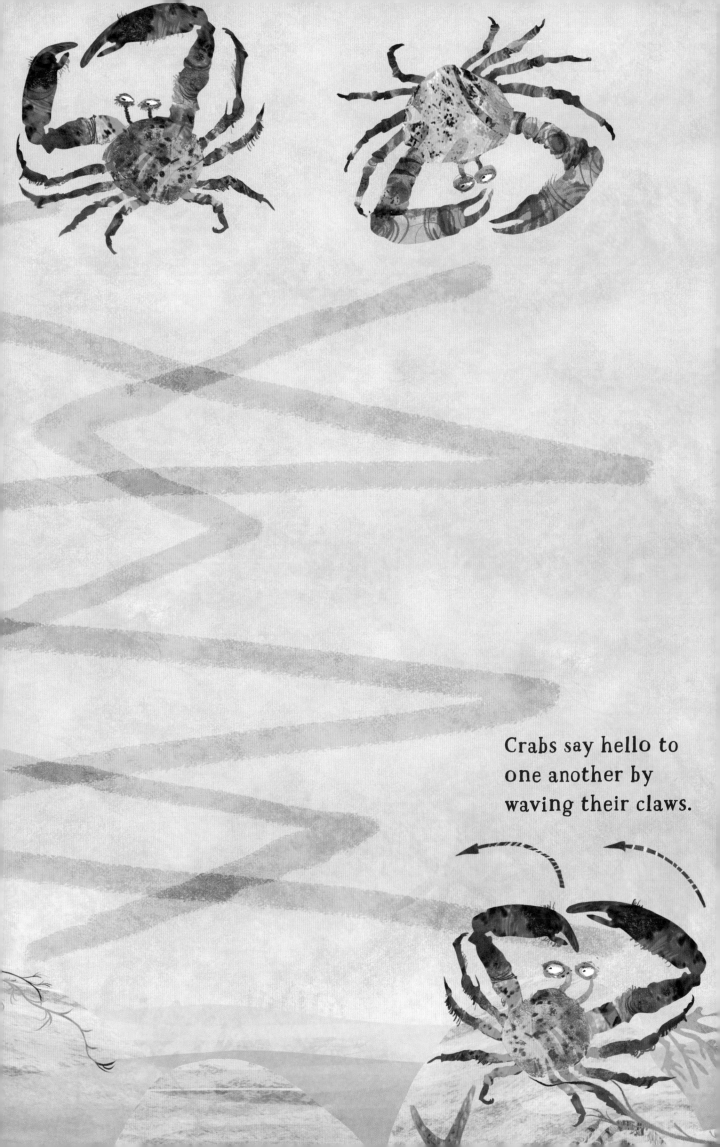

Crabs say hello to
one another by
waving their claws.

Seahorses have grippy tails like monkeys. They use them to hold themselves steady when the water is rough.

Stick seahorses onto this clump of seaweed so they don't get swept away by a strong wave.

Jellyfish move by shooting water out of their bodies. Draw the tentacles on these jellyfish to show which direction they're swimming in.

Dolphins love to race each other.
A spinner dolphin can turn 7 times
in the air! Circle the dolphin that
has won this spinning contest.

Draw more dolphins
racing under the water.

Coral reefs are home to lots
of special fish. Stick clownfish,
parrotfish, lionfish, boxfish
and surgeonfish in-between
the colorful coral.

Parrotfish

Coral is an animal too.
Color this coral for the
clownfish to hide in.

Surgeonfish

Boxfish

Lionfish

Play Boxfish Bingo
For two players

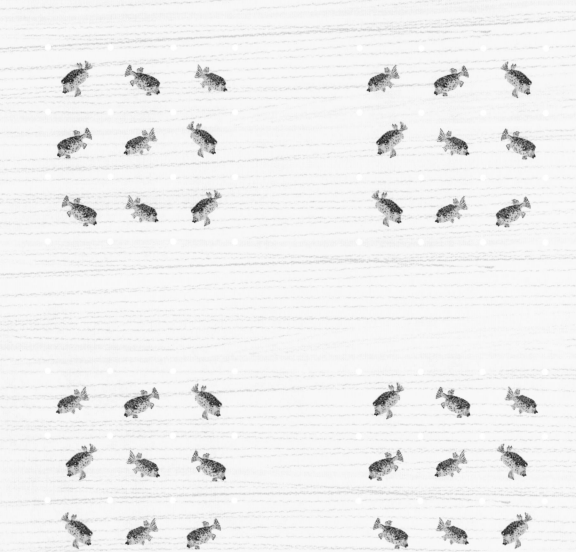

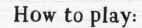

How to play:
Take turns drawing one line at a time between the white dots, each in a different color pen (no diagonal lines are allowed). When you complete a square in your color, write your initials inside it. The player with the most squares wins!

Color in these clownfish. Give them
bright orange bodies and white stripes.

Penguins have heavy bones
that help them dive deep
underwater for fish.

Stick penguins in the icy
Antarctic water. How many fish
will they catch for their dinner?

Deep-sea fish look very strange. They
have had to adapt in special ways to
living in the extreme cold and dark.

Design your own deep-sea fish.
What special features will it have?

Female anglerfish have a
light bulb hanging from their
heads. They gobble up fish
that are lured in by the light.

Ogrefish have sharp fangs that point inward so food can't escape from their mouths.

Gulper eels have big mouths and stretchy stomachs to catch as much food as possible.

Tide pools are left behind
when the tide goes out.
They are home to all sorts
of fascinating creatures.

Barnacles

Stick starfish in this
tide pool. Draw in other
creatures that you've
spotted at the beach.

Sea anemones

Mussels

Lemon sea slugs

Draw spots and stripes
on this seasnake.

Sea snakes have flat tails that they use
like rudders to speed through the water.

Eels have a long, ribbon-like
fins along their bodies. Circle
the eel on this page.

Octopuses have suckers
on their 8 tentacles to
help them catch food.

Stick some tasty
fish and prawns on
these octopuses'
tentacles.

Pufferfish scare predators away
by taking in water and puffing
themselves up into spiky balls.

Draw spikes on these pufferfish. Make their spikes extra sharp to scare off hungry predators!

Play Pop Goes the Pufferfish
For two players

Take it in turns to throw the dice. Move forward the number of space shown on the dice. The first player to reach the mussel shells wins.

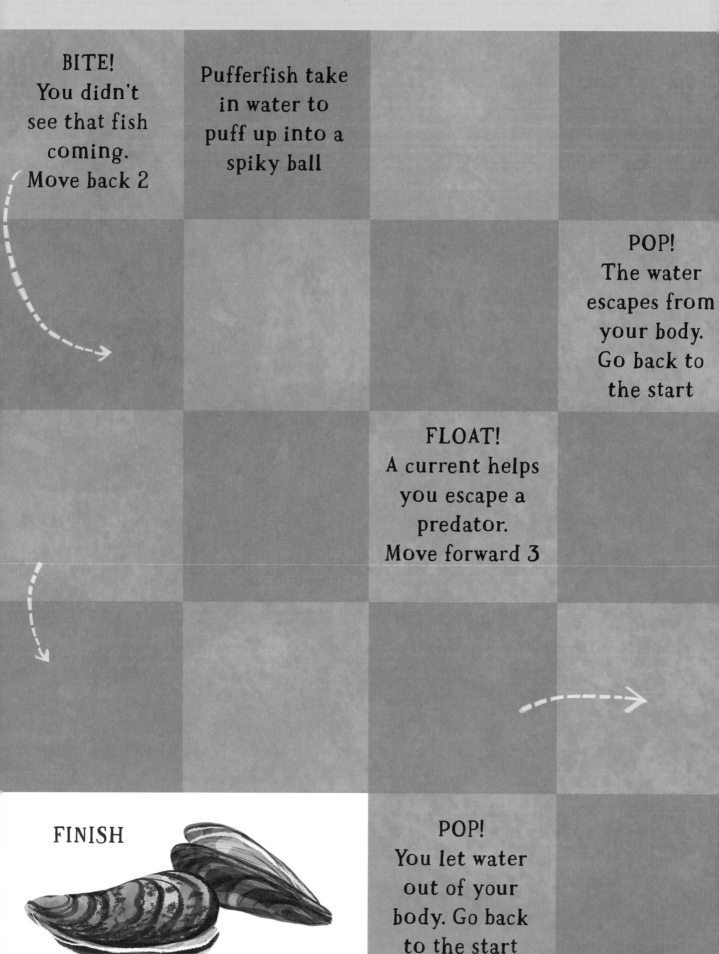

BITE!
You didn't see that fish coming. Move back 2

Pufferfish take in water to puff up into a spiky ball

POP!
The water escapes from your body. Go back to the start

FLOAT!
A current helps you escape a predator. Move forward 3

FINISH

POP!
You let water out of your body. Go back to the start

START

STING!
You sting a
predator.
Move forward 2

Pufferfish
are the most
poisonous fish
in the world

CATCH!
You find a
clam to eat.
Move forward 2

BITE!
You didn't
see that fish
coming...
Move back 2

Pufferfish
are very slow
swimmers.
Miss a go

Pufferfish prise
open shells
with their
beak-like lips

Humpback whales send messages to their friends by slapping the surface of the water.

Write whaley
messages in the
speech bubbles.

Blue whales can eat up to 4 tons of krill in one day. Draw krill in the tummy of this hungry blue whale.

Krill look a bit like shrimp.
At night, some types of krill
glow under the water.

Sea turtles have see-through
eyelids that they use like
swim goggles to see underwater.

Draw yourself swimming with
these sea turtles. Don't forget
your swim goggles and snorkel.

Sea turtles swim to shore to lay their eggs. Their eggs are made of a soft, bouncy material so they don't break when they hit the sand.

Draw eggs in these turtles' nests.

Seal pups know how to swim
as soon as they are born.
Stick playful seal pups in
the sea with this mother seal.

Seals can hold their breath
underwater for up to 2 hours!

Swordfish use their sharp and pointy noses to slash, spike and stun their prey.

Draw fish spiked on the nose of this swordfish.

Male dragonets perform a special frilly-fin dance to attract females.

Draw a line through this maze from this male dragonet fish to the female dragonet who is also sending out love signals.

Play Sardines and Tuna
For two players

How to Play:

Use sardine and tuna stickers
from the back of the book.
Each choose a type of fish.
Take turns placing your fish
on the grid. The first player
to get three fish in a row wins!

Play Spot the Difference

A stingray has poisonous spines in the middle of its tail. A mantra ray has no spines. Spot the odd ray out!

Deep-sea diving is one way
scientists can discover more
about animals who live in the sea.

Stick a special selection
of fish in the sea for
these divers to observe.

Color in the seaweed,
water weed and coral.

Test your knowledge of the BLUE

1. Which direction do crabs walk in?

2. How long can a seal hold its breath underwater?

3. What do blue whales mostly eat?

4. What does a female anglerfish have hanging from her head?

5. What is the most poisonous fish in the world?

Check the answers below to find out if you are an ocean expert.

Flying Fish

Seahorses

Prawns

Crabs

Krill

Starfish

Ogrefish

Jellyfish

Anglerfish

Seasnake

Swordfish

Dolphin

Tuna

Sardines

Clownfish

Parrotfish

Seaturtle

Boxfish

Dragonets

Penguins

Pufferfish

Shark

Seals

Octopus